Dear Parents/Caregivers:

Children learn to read in stages, and all children develop reading skills at different ages. **Fisher-Price® Ready Reader Storybooks™** were created to encourage children's interest in reading and to increase their reading skills. The stories in this series were written to specific grade levels to serve the needs of children from preschool through third grade. Of course, every child is different, so we hope that you will allow your child to explore the stories at his or her own pace.

All of the stories in this series are fun, easy-to-follow tales that have engaging full-color artwork. Children can move from books that have the simplest vocabulary and concepts, to each progressive level to expand their reading skills. With the **Fisher-Price® Ready Reader Storybooks™**, reading will become an exciting adventure for your child. Soon your child will not only be ready to read, but will be eager to do so.

Educational Consultants: Mary McLean-Hely, M.A. in Education: Design and Evaluation of Educational Programs, Stanford University; Wendy Gelsanliter, M.S. in Early Childhood Education, Bank Street College of Education; Nancy A. Dearborn, B.S. in Education, University of Wisconsin-Whitewater

Fisher-Price® Ready Reader Storybook™

No More Chores!

Written by Andrea Vuocolo • Illustrated by Tim Davis

Modern Publishing
A Division of Unisystems, Inc.
New York, New York 10022

"Come on, chicks!
There are chores awaiting.

There's work to do.
No more playing."

"Mama, dear, we want some fun.

Make a game for everyone."

"Follow me while we clean this place.

I'll put a smile on your face."

"The dolls and toys
have had their fun.
It's back in the toy chest
for everyone.

They will ride this wagon
back to their chest.
Load 'em up chicks!
They need a rest."

"A jump rope!
We can skip and rhyme.
A puzzle for some
quiet time.

The wagon is loaded.
It is ready to go.
I think someone is
missing, though."

"Mister Bunny is not around.
Wait, did I hear a sound?"

"*Help, I'm lost!*"
"Do you hear it, too?
Let's go see what we
can do."

"Smooth that sheet.
Tug that blanket.
Pull that bedspread–
Really yank it.

Out pops Bunny,
floppity-flip.
Put him in the wagon,
in time for the trip."

"Let's go, chicks!
It's time to roll.
Join the pet and plant patrol.

We will take some seeds.
We will spread them out.
Dig and prune and
give a shout."

"Back inside to feed the fish.
Look at their colors.
Make a wish.

Tap the fish food.
Watch it sink.
I guess HE doesn't
need a drink!"

"The plants get water.
Now they'll grow.
It always makes me
wonder, though.

It isn't tasty. It doesn't crunch.
Is it a bath? Or is it lunch?"

"And here we are, at
our last stop.

Circle around the tabletop."

"The table is set.
Please take a seat.

CREAM

Pass me your bowls.
It is time for a treat!"